**Kristin Hersh** is a musician, author, mother of four and founder of the seminal art rock band Throwing Muses. Over three decades she has also performed as a solo artist and leader of 50FootWave, released dozens of critically acclaimed albums, and written her memoirs, *Rat Girl*, *Paradoxical Undressing* and *Don't Suck, Don't Die*. Kristin currently lives in California.

With thanks to the Patron of this book
S J Watson


**Also by the author**

*Rat Girl*
*Paradoxical Undressing*
*Don't Suck, Don't Die*

crooked // bright yellow gun // hot pink,
distorted // Mississippi kite // delicate
cutters // wax // and a she-wolf after the
war // pretty ugly // pearl // America //
shimmer // flipside // medicine rush // San
Franci

# kristin hersh

serene
// sta                                     gun //
the field // spring // shotgun // Listerine //
white trash moon // skeleton key // no way in
hell // snake oil // sand // glass cats //
golden

# nerve endings

// The
Thin M                                     eye //
Deep Wilson // Sunray Venus // finished // your
dirty answer // power and light // Clark's
nutcracker // snailhead // baseball field //
civi

# selected lyrics

Sno-
Cat                                     d //
faith // radiant addict // Juno // status quo
// bubble net // cold water coming // teeth //
echo // Milk St. // two step // pneuma // buzz
// Milan // husk // William's cut // catch //
cathedral heat // Clara Bow // me and my charms
// St. Christopher // diving bell // smoky
hands // animal // red shoes // krait // soma
gone slapstick // between Piety and Desire //
colder // dripping trees // killing two birds
// long painting // limbo // Ginger Park //
Arnica Montana // same sun // Candyland // you
cage // caffeine // gazebo tree // vitamins v
// say goodbye // him dancing // a cleaner
light // Mexican wor        // God's not a dick
// clay feet // from        plane // 37 hours //
hips and makers // crooked // bright yellow

unbound

First published in 2018
This paperback edition first published in 2021

Unbound

Level 1, Devonshire House, One Mayfair Place, London W1J 8AJ

www.unbound.com

Text design by Patty Rennie

A CIP record for this book is available
from the British Library

ISBN 978-1-80018-035-2 (trade pbk)
ISBN 978-1-78352-563-8 (trade hbk)
ISBN 978-1-78352-564-5 (ebook)
ISBN 978-1-78352-565-2 (limited edition)

Printed in Great Britain by Clays Ltd, Elcograf S.p.A

1  2  3  4  5  6  7  8  9

This book is dedicated to my bandmates
and to all people who listen

# Contents

# Introduction

People close to me would always feel it first. My brother would touch my arm and know, my husband would sit bolt upright in bed, my bandmates'd flinch and try to rub it off. Songs start as electricity, hair standing on end, skin buzzing . . . suddenly you can see with your skin; it's weird. Auras come next, as the players in the material glow and ask to come to life. And then the noise: a jagged chattering that set my teeth on edge and, yet, I couldn't stop following it. Gross, but still fascinating; the kind of gross you *can't* look away from. It's Robert Johnson's crossroads, where the personal and collective unconscious meet, God's and the Devil's Venn diagram, saints and sinners, etc.

I'm making it sound dramatic, but it was more like Bigfoot in the underbrush. Such a weird animal and nobody really believes you saw him. My photographs of him were blurry at best, proof that I was a crazy redneck.

It still embarrasses me. That the jagged chattering becomes words I have to stick in my mouth and spit out. *People can hear it.* That the stories the songs tell are all mine . . . ugh. I'm so very shy. But Bigfoot the guy isn't as shy as hiding in the underbrush would imply. He *poses* for those blurry pictures. All primates are social.

Over the years, the many years, of hiding in tour-bus bunks and motel bathtubs, sneaking into basements, attics, backyards and the back seats of cars — clandestine meetings with music — I've come to see the love in love/hate. It's the part without fear, where your eyes and ears and skin and heart settle on the truth and you *can't* look away. So you don't. That's love. Cuz hate is only fear. I'm not afraid any more because pain and horror and cruelty are just shadows of their opposites, everybody standing at the crossroads, not just God and the Devil, but all of us and our angels and archangels. Fucking creepy and yet still a party. I mean, don't get me wrong: our poor hearts. But still . . . we're *here* and as far as we know, this is the place to be.

I'm in another poorly lit dressing room right now, typing instead of playing guitar. I know that when I open the Tele case at my feet, spirits will fly out, some better intentioned than others. But the songs they sing aren't mine. The songs *I* sing aren't mine. They're just Bigfoot posing, being social, coming to the party and leaving early while we all look at each other and ask, "Who was that?" I still don't know, really. All I have are these photographs and, like I said, they aren't mine. They were taken for *you*, though they aren't for everyone. I like them, probably love them, but I only took them to pass along to the other social primates hiding in the underbrush, standing at the crossroads, ducking into the back seat to see with their skin.

# nerve endings

## crooked

hold the flashlight under your chin
closer as the lights dim

you lonely doll
you lucky dog
you free fall down to the living room

closer as the lights dim

spread the glitter on your pillow
count your blessings on your fingers
crawl your way back down the stairs
down to the living room

closer as the lights dim

glittering in La-Z-Boys and Christmas lights
glittering
then found a dark body to the right and crooked

# bright yellow gun

with your bright yellow gun
you own the sun
and i think i need a little poison

to keep me tame
keep me awake

i have nothing to offer but confusion and the
    circus in my head
in the middle of the bed
in the middle of the night

with your bright silver frown
you own the town
and i think i need a little poison

i have no secrets
i have no lies
i have nothing to offer but the middle of the night
and i think you need a little poison

## hot pink, distorted

it'll take much more than water to fix my hot pink,
    distorted face
and more than self hypnosis to believe it doesn't
    taste like gasoline

i was not invited back

here comes the thunder
there goes the rain

you poor misguided soldier
ugly daughters show no mercy
in the heat of battle these brats'll feel no pain

quick and dirty they take you down

here comes the thunder
there goes the rain

# Mississippi kite

you paint your own tv on the wall
carve out insects to feed us all
lights flash by and the fast world echoes your
    thoughts

your compass led you to the edge of a lake
you'll singe your nuts down there if you take such
    bad advice from the love gods of hate
you'll get cold

you get burned
you get cold

on the plush green rug in the lime green light
eyes like white stones in black light
i promise you everything that you like
i go, "Mississippi kite"

gloss assails us
then dims
comic book nights
LA grim
the Hollywood Martians, lucky stiffs, fucking win

you told me enough times you can't give me enough
   rope to hang myself one time
but i can always hope you come down on me so hard
   that i choke and go

you get burned
you get cold

meanwhile, i feed you boric acid and air, lemon
   drops, snow cream, speckled eggs
the sweat seeps into a crack in your head and you
   go, "Mississippi kite"

# delicate cutters

it's just the lack of time i keep
reaching out
lashing at

it's just the lines run down the walls
i can't believe they never fall
the walls never leave
and the walls begin to scream
and my toes against the wall
i stare ahead
the door inside the wall
your face inside the door
you crawl across the room

the picture never moves
my boots are very still
you slide to my feet
you slide across the floor

i throw your head across the ice
i throw my hands through the window
crash
like poetry

it's four o'clock
i'm waiting
your face appears
i keep forgetting your name
while i'm writing this you crash through the wall
you fall off the floor

a room full of delicate cutters all sitting down
the room has many doors
all but one of them are closed
she goes around locking all the doors
this has another ending full of innocent children
all but one of them are closed

this has another ending
full of delicate cutters
opening the doors

**wax**

just look at the pictures and the spring
    cleaning debris
stumbling into something more moving than biology

red mullets are only red under stress
pale pink otherwise
but cherry ice and blue paint are chemical debris
stumbling into something more brutal than biology
wax in your ears
wax in mine

then heads roll and heads roll

lashed by wet ponytails
you're seasick, brittle and grim
stumbling into something more brutal than
    chemical debris
wax in your ears
wax in mine

# and a she-wolf after the war

so it's cowboys in flying colors riding home
leave my tears alone
it's too funny

it's me and she spilling jewels and collarbones

i can see them riding over the hills
cowboy hats are back in
this is the future after the war and i don't
    need anymore

Frank Lloyd Wright
try to sleep under a dome under the sky

# pretty ugly

pretty ugly
uncivilized
kisses blow in the filmy wind
i feed off the mood you're in

faces alert
bodies slack
we drone like the flies around us
you can't see the sky from here

i'll take you at your word: we got away with
    murder
look up: a clear blue sky

i'm alone in the gleaming whiteness
you drone through your dirty secrets
and when i wake up you'll be gone

i love you like a bitch's son but it's too late to
    trust anyone

## pearl

hot hands move things
i write on his wall
i have no mind at all

hot things move him
i write on his wall
i have no heart at all

i think she's a pretty little fool
she holds me down
she flows
she has a back like Marie

i think he's a crazy bastard
drives me home
he goes, you have a back like Marie
you have pearls on your eyes

and you use your burning to wrap yourself in
and you use your fever to hide yourself away
and you use your sweating to keep me down
and you use your heat to have me
and you use your fire to be stronger than me
and you use your flame against me

i won't come back like Marie
the pearls on my eyes
these pearls on my eyes
they make me blind

i write on your wall
i have no eyes at all

# America

follow the road
swallow a snake
find shoes in the corner
run away

he had a nightmare
i'm losing my person
i'm only talking

but look at me
i'm in bed
i'm asleep
i'm a mess

she can't say America
can't say no
she can't stand up

## shimmer

you in the water underneath the tarp
it don't rain under the water
it don't rain inside my heart

don't follow me home

you walking in the Gulf Stream
tail between your legs
it's not funny
if you ask me it's just funny in your head

hang on

my tongue is filled with sugar and my back is filled
    with pain
your tongue is on my shoulder and there's nothing
    on my brain

don't follow me home

shake barrels of whiskey down my throat
i'll still see straight
ride out on a pony
even loose i won't be late

# flipside

there's always drooling zombies or at least
   one dick
i'm having trouble focusing 'cause all i see in
   front of me is you when we're finally alone

he was the bone king
dead to all the world
maybe dead's like being really high without the
   low but i enjoy the hangovers here

i could see them on the flipside of a molecule
but i have all the energy i can take for now
holy floating
we're holy floating

holy shit
i think i'd rather be on the ground than flying
we're still fucking up in a healthy way for now

how dare you save my life then try to break
   my heart?
you make alone so goddamn lonely
makes me wanna fall in love with everything and
   float above the ground

these days i do the same thing
commit the same damn crime
if i'm not feeling out the flipside
maybe i'm supposed to be here
maybe you're supposed to be here, too?

and my feet don't touch the ground

## medicine rush

behind the liquor store i break down
and in some fucking body's safe house
we're not the way we intended us
not even close

medicine rush or clarifier?
dangerous candy or safe fire?
you're supposed to be the first to go
not the last one standing

you coming undone is gorgeous
spewing in the hot wind like a virus

# San Francisco

breakfast at the movies
Gatorade and blackjack on the bed
God bless the ugly
cheap champagne and blackjack on the bed

i was born in America
born with the fists of a saint
way out of range

breakfast in the hallway
pistachios and cocktails on the roof
God bless the hard way
you're the only easy substitute

i was born in America
born with the fists of a cowboy
home on the range

## Rubidoux

the freeway's freeway close
i laugh from the back
the race is over

headlights on your teeth race down both your backs
in the dark blue car
a party

blue trash on the floor
i hope you find your hunger in a hungry world

# honeysuckle

honeysuckle voodoo
smoke under the door of this hotel room
how did you find me?
spooky mojo and divining rod

a soggy mounting hope
you take it out
you take it out, it glows

i'd rather be fucking than fighting
anyway
they're the same
i'd rather be fucking than talking
anyway
they're both confusing

sodium popper
it's getting darker and darker
your temples throb with effort and your notes hit
    every target hard

this solution
your hired hands say it's ok

## serene

sun bakes the window makes the sheets hot and wet
at night they're cold and blue
why do i like you?
'cause i do

why do i like you?
'cause i'd kill to be you
sweet nothing
sweet dreams
serene

dancing with scissors
our bones fill of wishes
we wait for our plans to come true
why do i like you?
'cause i do

we fill each other's arms
you wanna wish higher?
you wanna live higher?
lose control

if you're in the ballpark then you can play
    the game
you know you know the rules
why do i like you?
'cause i'm thrilled to be here
sweet nothing
sweet dreams
serene

## static

your mouth fell out of the sky and suddenly i had
    it memorized
but honestly?
it's like you're dead

a pretty picture of you breathing air and you're
    just standing there
static

your hope is on the wing is on a bus tearing down
    the road
your road is in the dark is in the sun in the rain
    and cold
you're cold
you're made of heat
you're made of skin
made of cloth and bone
your bones are made of sponge are made of
    Plexiglas, tin and hope

## your ghost

if i walk down this hallway tonight
it's too quiet
so i pad through the dark and call you on
   the phone
push your old numbers and let your house ring
'til i wake your ghost

let him walk down your hallway
it's not this quiet
slide down your receiver
sprint across the wire
follow my number
slide into my hand

it's the blaze across my nightgown
it's the phone's ring

i think last night
you were driving circles around me

i can't drink this coffee 'til i put you in
   my closet
let him shoot me down
let him call me off
i take it from his whisper
you're not that tough

# under the gun

my heart goes out to you
a lover on a night with no moon

i learned to fill out gaunt limbs like the parrot
    lady at Lake Michigan
troubled by a troubled life
we hover, blurry and glassy-eyed

we passed this way before
we said this then
under the gun
we run

my heart goes out to you
your puny savings blown

the parrot lady and the Bali mask
a boy steps carefully over the grass
the lizard looking up at me is so goddamn Disney

## the field

wait
you just wait
we're lost again

great
aw, just great
we're lost again

get your mouth out of the gutter
get your butt back to the sand
if it gets any hotter
rock your baby in the sun and make your big break
we're us again

shake your big weight
you'll crave again

the field has melted snow in summer
black with lousy rain
one more star above the clouds is not such a
    bad thing
i have to say
one more star above the boys is not such a
    bad thing

say it
just say
we're safe again

## spring

nothing like chrome when it shines
no better weather to drive
if you squint you can see it
if you limp you can reach it

all i want is spring
all i want is you smiling

all i want is green
all i want is you smiling

faithful to the finish
i'm grateful to be in this with you
a fucker of a lifeline
a mother of a lifetime with you

## shotgun


i called shotgun
our car submerged
your breakneck speed slowed to a float

out on a thalidomide limb
truncated
stiff as a board
delinquent no more

can't see the fog for the trees
i lost my way on reject beach
lost my heart
lost it

you can't live until you die

i called shotgun
our car submerged
your breakneck speed slowed
two afloat

# Listerine

Listerine covers your tracks
doesn't do shit for the facts

i'm lying on the couch
scary memories fill my mouth

how did i love a breaking thing?
how did i sleep through a kidnapping?
how'd i trust a band who'd leave me one by one?

i only wanted the spark
i only wanted your hearts
i only wanted the high
wasn't much more to my life

i couldn't wait to come down
there's nothing here but the ground

## white trash moon

the neighbors' dog won't let you sleep
try not to stare at the neighbors' hair

out of the chaos
my us
and your daddy's fingernail

ten thousand miles of moonscape
don't keep anybody away after all
close to the source on a white trash moon
under the horny sun of July

the neighbors' gun won't let you sleep
try not to stare at their underwear

out of the chaos
my us
and the coyote's lonely wail

## skeleton key

grab me
grab your skeleton key
and don't forget to breathe

waste of space

grab me
and don't forget to breathe

## no way in hell

love's got this drag on it
no way in hell would i turn to you know too
    damn much
no way in hell

you sold my clothes to those girls
drink 'til i'm numb then i'm gone
say goodnight

i sleep with one hand on my clothes
i sleep with one hand on my heart
there's almost nothing left
left to guard

for each time i say goodbye
i swallow you once every night
say goodnight

no way in hell would i give
no way in hell would i fold
no way in hell would i burn
no way in hell would i go

## snake oil


well i never
i never saw anybody move like that before

why do we spend so much time here on the floor
looking up like i did before your intoxicating
   movement
ate away at my sad eyes and my headache?

i never
i never thought i'd be falling
i'd be caught

i see a bone and a straw in the dirt-white
   Nevada light
i squint against his shirt
my sleeping pills melted and i sleep fine
the tears on my shoulder won't keep me up tonight

the snake around my finger starts to unwind

soak up the weather
suck up the sun
into your bones
then move on

## sand

race through the country
the perfect carnivore
pull over and stop to breathe
there's grape jelly on your sleeve

you pick me up
i pull you down
down to the ground

make the most of daylight
a sun drenched meadow by the dumpster
i came back high and hungover from your
    flickering light

i hope you find your way home to the country
the perfect manifested heaven
and stop to breathe
there's an aching heart on your sleeve

your brain unbuckled: luxurious and softer
    than sand

## glass cats

so leave the bottom feeders to their old shrines
we'll hang in heaven with our own kind

Sunday morning sleet
just a little mercy
boy, you make it shine

outside is blue
in this house is golden
boy, you make it shine

## golden ocean

your baby takes your balls and gives you back
    your teeth
your baby takes your balls and lights a fire in
    your belly

a sweaty pepper thing
how do we keep it clean?
no snow
no rain
how do you expect to keep this place clean?

LA
sugar pills make bitter spit and glitter skin
then golden sugar skin
sugar skin and the golden ocean

your baby joins your party
kicks you out the door
your baby is your Mardi Gras in glitter and
    confetti

## flood

fly
you get high, right?
fly
and you get high, right?

try
you'll get by alright
try
and you'll get by alright

Ry
you're my bright light
you're my bright light

oh god, i'm high

waterfalls of light
flood my eyes with light
flood my eyes with my aching eyesight

my aching eyes

# devil's roof

i have two heads
where's the man?
he's late

one burns
one's sky
where's the man?
he's late

i'm two headed
one free
one sticky

but is it freedom can burn?
is sticky ever blue?
for instance: where's my husband?

this is what i need
why i can't stay
god, this is the devil
too bad he's late
i love the smell of beer
the smell of dark
the feel of dark
to feel the rug
to press the rug beneath me
a small party

but is it sinners can burn?
i hear we let them speak
for instance: where's my husband?

dance on the devil's roof under a devil's moon
i don't care and you don't move

## The Thin Man

we're just a little starving
two feet away and i can't reach
two feet away like a dream

you rub your hands together
sparks fly
the thin man and his hungry wife

fireworks for you in the sirocco
fire works for you in the ozone snow

we're just a little lonely
did you break a promise half asleep?
did you make a promise can't keep?

## hook in her head


certain things i love spend my time
i guess i'll have to unhook those hooks

this woman literally felt she had a hook in
  her head

rip it up
live it down
make it big
keep it clean
shake it off
take him home
take it off
do him good
keep it up
shake it off


he's a fucking drag but if you don't then you
  watch him go
if you can you see it home
you be strong
and when you die
it's a shame
but your old life stays the same

she has a hook in her head

i saw this lady close her eyes
the bottle slipped between her fingers and slid
    along the aisle

if i were a man i'd have a gun
but i'm so bone tired
i'm so bone tired
i'm old

i watch the snow make slow time
i watch the snow cover up the bottle so i can
    slip between
i'll read the label from underneath

## lazy eye

it might be electrical
i left a broken impression anyway
it might be blood or Coke on the front step of
   Store 24

keep your lazy eye in line
sometimes we see so clearly with tears in our eyes

you whisper warm space advice

you always had it in for me
steeped in earthly and otherworldly tragedy
shake it off or go back to sleep

sometimes we see so clearly with fear in our eyes

# Deep Wilson


slipping down railings and balconies with a
    sleepy ease i never knew
i navigate my way to you

indigent darkness
thick as a dream
a liquid party underneath
though i'm still shaky and weak

knees pressed against the leather couch
i couldn't find my bra
and you were so familiar i think that i leaned out
    too far
i wouldn't have if my heart and my stomach hadn't
    fallen so hard

that's some hat trick
an effortless move
that tearful frantic creature seems far away
    from here

my New Orleans nickel ring
your Deep Wilson tattoo
under your bullshit radar i came to find you

## Sunray Venus


unfrightened, careless
unfrightened, blank
we sit at the young man's feet
mouths working
and no one remembers to pray

working in dull light
another island
where no one remembers to pray

open your mouth
you're blessed for the moment
kisses all around
Sunray Venus crushed underfoot and kisses
    all around
leaving that is limbo
hell, i remember you

touched, withered, crushed in a moment
brought your body down
slid your brain around

that's some disease you got there
a lousy friend
pour your heart out at his feet
crying, puking
still, no one remembers your name

feel your way through sound
another island
where no one remembers your name

## finished

with a loud noise everything breaks
everything falls
rips open
leaves a hole

follow the black moonlit
follow the passing gaze
alone at last
bury it inside
bury it
come home

his wife dying
he saw her face: rebuked, refused
coming home

left it outside
left it
goodbye
he wants
tears he cries
"i cannot say goodbye"
finished

hope is a dog
don't spin me around again
your face
it paragraphs
caught in a gape
a hole

found a year
found another year

when we sit at a table
there's fire between the gaps
when your hands don't touch there's sand in
    your face
and fire under your nails

nobody knew
so nobody cared
nobody knows

## your dirty answer

you know how it feels when the real world
    encroaches
rubbing elbows with the unemployed and you
you're so beautiful
you're so rude

peeling mangoes on a fold out couch
i'm scooped out
you're inscrutable
you're all mine

swimming is a 'lude
wine opens your mind
your guitar's a race car
sex is your best friend
what's your dirty answer?

my fantasies are unlived histories
you know what it's like when mistakes go unmade
it was beautiful
it was you

i'm giving up the ugly i thought you'd make pretty
i'll be goddamned
this is beautiful
hold my hand

i don't judge people
i just watch them 'til it's time to look away
i wanna look away now
somebody's coming

i don't wanna live backwards
i don't wanna even look backwards
it's not my fault
it's not my fault you don't love me
it's not my fault you don't love me when i'm drunk

i'm wiped
i'm so tired
carry me for a little while

## power and light

it's getting later and later

power and light purring soft and low
a pilot light burning

it's getting later and later

silence is eloquent, too, and kind
hearts thrust into heartbreak soup

desperate times call for desperate pleasures
if you must
then degrade

traveling souls like us
the wicked
the carnies
we all eat up this swill
these fucked bedtime stories

desperate times call for desperate pleasures
if you must degrade
do it quiet

power and light purring soft and low
a pilot light burning

it's getting later and later

# Clark's nutcracker


snap our skulls shut
spark off yesterday
phantom brain headaches

such a loud laugh in the platinum sun
the platinum blasted sun

'cause you're, uh, wired
you just crumple up
you just tumble down, don't you?
i mean, you know you do

said a mouthful through a mouthful of ginger ale
    and love
lift our platinum son
us two shall pass
we're made of glass

it's complicated
you just crumple up
you just hunker down, don't you?
i mean, you know you do

## snailhead


is it enough to grow old?
is there enough to go around?
to have a box in my snailhead?
i don't know

and a diamond growing old under the ocean that's
    as black as where you came from
black as rocks
as the box inside your head
what did they do?
where is the ocean so black?

don't say the circle's broken
and the diamond: smoke

what did they do?
we can't be wrong
where did it break?
the fucking spiral was a circle
we are gone

spot on the sun
where have you gone?
what have i done?

## baseball field


lovely empty baseball field
just one of the places to sun
like a hot pink kite with no string
heads rolling
you make heads roll

whistle today away
whistle one day away
you make headway

drift 'til the stuff that you're breathing seems
    like air
you go back there

lovely empty baseball field
just one of the places set your lawn chair
like a hummingbird with no wings
heads rolling
you have time and baby oil shine

whisper today away
whisper one day away
you make headway

drift 'til a piece of a place nests in your hair
you go back there

talking at the radio
just one of the places to shoot off your mouth
like a hot summer dog on a lawn
here today
never gone

## nerve endings

nerve endings mutiny
put a rock into my brain
i feel almost everything

could you ever really live in a house?
could you ever live in a body?
just chicken i guess
just chicken i know
but radiantly so

nerve endings think they see pleasure coming
i know better

put a rock into my brain
i feel almost everything

## civil disobedience

sick with amazement
i'm soaking and broke

"here's a big fat aspirin
maybe you'll choke"

"that's not funny"

i don't like you any more than you know
but i still like you too much

this city's insane
these people are crazy
you can buy me breakfast and then find me a coat
back in that apartment i saw too many ghosts to
    go home

this bread is old
my coffee's cold
we live on toast and coffee
we live on bread and water
we live on Coke and pretzels
we live on bread and water

## Tuesday night


when you sleep you tell me off
i told you once before
i can't resist you

when you sleep i build you up
i make you king of here
i can't resist you

i can't wait

i'll suck down another water while i wait
i watch the clock glow blue and think of you

i can't wait

the moon shines through my dress and through
   my glass
i promise not to drink until you're home
i can't wait

the moon pales even when it thinks it holds the
   face of the clock i watch for you

## Sno-Cat

a man made of butterfat careening around on a
    Sno-Cat
and i can't drive any faster
my hands are like ice and the moon shines on
    pepper trees and road grease
the yellow lines look blue

snow buries Whitehall
white powdered Nembutal and i can't think anymore
my feet are like ice as the moon sets on Christmas
    trees and plastic deer

i thank god you're comatose as i pull back the
    bedclothes
and i can't believe my composure
and i can't remember my anger

and summer is a fish story
i wonder where we'll be

## Bath white

and on the way down
wait it out
and on the sand: rotten apples
and what you had: only shadows

i wasn't brutal
i wasn't anything at all
consensus or confession
i don't recognize depression

and all day you flaunt your addictions, buddy
as your crowd gathers around

no matter who you are
no matter what you wanted
drugstore glare lights your path
damp memories fill your head
bath white glare lights your path
damp memories still your hand

and all night you court your attraction to me
like a surfer high on the ground

no matter who you are
no matter what you wanted

and on the way down
wait it out
and on the sand was rotten apples
and what you caught was only shadows

## furious

you're furious

i never taught you to sing
you carry rocks in your head and pitch them
    without warning
happy drunk

you're furious

i beg you for sin
i beg your skin
you buy a whore
don't give her water

# Wonderland

you said aloud:
"i'm not allowed
i'm in trouble"

under your breath:
"i got one left in me
i'm in trouble"

you step outside and hydrogen pops again
on the white hot sidewalk
thunder and Wonderland gone

you had it all
you're losing her
losing
you're lost

you run and hide

## faith

was it me or the cold made you give up hope
made you lose your faith in the afterlife and all
   she made?

was it me or the heat made you not believe
made you lose your faith in the afterlife and all
   that breathes?

# radiant addict

so this is God's country
boy, his bugs are itchy
and does the day stretch out before you like
   the meadow
endless and followed by another day?

maybe i'm spineless
maybe i lack backbone
some things you don't forget:
a look that said forgive me
oh yeah
followed by another look

you hopeless addict
you radiant addict

you wake up on the diving board
you wake up
the sky black
head full of crap

and does the day stretch out?
so saw the moment in half
don't leave the party early

# Juno

i can't play when he wakes up
she said
he can't play when he thinks i'm growing up

that song, Juno, they did in the street
so many places to go and not one for me
said the she

that song, Juno, they sung in the street
her husband of nineteen years danced madly at
   her feet

now i can be balancing

## status quo

i dreamed you saw the eyes of a paranoid man
and quit your vision of the millennium
leaving our hope in the hands of the psychics

peace isn't quiet
i'm heading down the freeway
i'm hanging on the frequency of your voice
i'm drunk on the sound of your voice

i dreamed i climbed a hill in the midnight mud
and you turned a blind eye to the baby
leaving our hope in the hands of the psychos

there are sapphires in the trees
and the moths as big as bats
lucky me to have all that

what do you have on your mind?

## bubble net


inspired weakness under sleepy sun
and one cloud is a meltdown

there's no tomorrow

bang a left a bubble net waits over the next
    threshold
wearing tear stains
hovering over your shame
syringes scatter below
your body freight
baptize your weight
let it go past the next plateau

## cold water coming

that filthy stare
he's on a tear
cold water coming for the warm water junkies

i found a friend
lost him again
poor sucker freaked and couldn't swim with
    the monkeys

away
gone away
to your still house
in your still house you fall into icy blue
    cold water

**teeth**


i could get a piece of meat from a barren tree
nothing ever spoiled on me

you brought this, you dipshit
nothing ever spoiled on me

that cloud stomps around my house
does whatever it pleases
it teases me
what the hell?

never was a baritone 'til you stepped in
never dried my halters on the line
this hairdo's truly evil
i'm not sure it's mine

you're so tall
it's like i climb a waterfall

## echo

white label on the back seat glows an artificial
   green
i crave a midnight something
i crave and something hunts me down
i'm scaring everybody
i'm wearing everybody down

white label on the back seat
and something bends me over down
i crave an empty lifestyle
i crave the very loudest sound
i'm chasing everybody
i'm shaking everybody down

do you hear the loudest sound and you and me in
   the echo?

white label on the back seat
and something warm across my lap
i never bitched at anyone
i never asked for my heart back
i'm loving everybody and hating everyone i see

do you still remember me floating out on the echo?

## Milk St.

you are good
you are kind
you are drunk all the time
but never drunk enough

as you're battered by the underside of what we
    swore we wanted
and bothered by the crapshoot that has put you
    half to sleep
a sorely needed sleep

i'll hang outside the door all night
i'll bang on the door all night

you are good
you are brave
no matter what you say
but never brave enough

## two step

two step behind the rest
one fingertip too long
a hole in the box they carry spills sugar in
    the road

pour dimes in Diamond Jim
two months to fill him in

## pneuma

did i just hear you try to lemon scent the sky?
sulphur
yellow sulphur
yellow sky

i tongue a socket and you feel the jolt
you're like a warped godmother with your
    baffling love

i know what's in the air

you know what?
shut the fuck up

a spoonful of sugar
a labor of love
pneuma and pollution don't confuse me any

aquamarine and video green
hot water and pink soap
our teeth full of holes and our guts full of holes
thighs stick to hot vinyl

cringing through life wedgies
i strain to hear you over the brainless chattering
    null set

## buzz

fell out of the sky
i fell out of the sky
checked the time

while you wait for your clothes to dry
i cut lemons and lemons and limes

one sour finger
pretty as a picture
i always have a smile for you

i need a boat can cut through the swamp and take
    you for a ride
you need a suit for jaunts through the swamp
your clothes never dried

the boys change my name
i'm flying again
my limes make a baby healthy and wise
i cut lemons and lemons and limes

don't worry the bees
they buzz around me
don't worry the bees
the buzz sounds sweet to me

# Milan

what makes you gold-flecked?
you talk backwards like i do
hold still
your cold voodoo just slapped her upside the head

blood squeezed through your veins
you wear memories as false pain
who better than you to bless her
baptize the dead?

all's fair in New Orleans
so spend the night whispering
can't stand the heat?
get out of here
warm blooded
cold hearted
you can't finish what you started
can't stand the heat?
get out of here

clear sailing
murky water
you're still the smoothest talker
all twisted up
ham fisted

you don't want the devil's daughter
wasted
inebriated
you don't want her but you brought her here

one step backward
you lost your way
your haunted virtue
you threw it away

# husk

terrible wine set you free
damn slap happy sleep
c'mon out
c'mon out

oh mercy
mercy me

terrible wine draws you out
damn slap happy in the dugout
c'mon down
c'mon down

oh mercy
mercy me

and when you're smoke
how do you speak?
smoke signals?
write on trees?

# William's cut

it was all passion misunderstood
all passion mislaid
i'm on a mission by mistake and i hate it
i lost every friend i ever made

but i like it too much
i like it too much
i like it
and junkie hearts are broken

how many times can you get fucked in how many
    different ways?
you separate the good guys from disaster and it's
    even sadder
i lost every hope i ever had

sand stings your face and i wanted you back
your shell starts to crack
fits you like a glove
sand stings your face and i wanted you back
your heart's out of whack

it's you under a spell for a change

## catch

catch a bullet in your teeth
i put my head in the sand
oh boy

hi
bad, big bridges
big, big buildings
blue boy

it's raining out here
it's freezing out here

catch a bullet in your head
i put my teeth in the sand
oh boy

## cathedral heat


arrest the boy
warm between the eyes
as he jackknifes into winter

stung like a cutthroat trout in the cathedral heat

arrest the boy
the hayseed with the song in his heart
as he writhes through the winter

well, i forget what it's like to be kissing in the
    middle of a terrible dream
i forget what it's like to be kissing in the
    middle of a terrible storm
what a terrible thing

## Clara Bow

i didn't use you but i wish i had
i never liked you but i wish i did

whether it was soaking in poppy tea or your
    Southern hospitality
your voice has a sing-song quality and bones were
    made to be broken

yes
alright
i can
with sunburned lips i can bitch
about another stupid summer

paste eaters like this sad season
strong women gripe and bite your heavy tongues

## me and my charms

you can come back when you want
just know that i'll be here
i haven't left this step

and when the lights go out
i pick the angel up
i only have two hands

is she here?
is she here right now?
drive her off
don't bother to call
i'm checking out today

me and my charms
when i kiss the angel
i have a taste of you
when i take the angel
i have a piece of you

you can come back
i haven't left you yet

## St. Christopher

blow out the candle so he can't see in the window
smoke fills the tiny room
sweat home
high
we can fool around
fight off the smell of doom

you smell like cold and dry leaves
leaving is hardest on hookworm sidewalks
just snow static on the crap tv
fluorescent exposure
a gold grin told her Christ's not saving the weak

i wanna go faster
i wanna go farther from home

dang
flag's at quarter mast
even though i fed and slept you
paced the foamy sand
crawled in the back seat
our friends all broke
unmoved by unspent youth
you still damp with foam and hungry

# diving bell

on the way
you blab like a happy bimbo
sifting the night air for weapons before you suck
    it into your lungs

into the diving bell with foraging behemoths
to a snow blown motel and beachcombing behemoths

on the way
you blush like a raving psycho
tossing a mussel back to life before you suck us
    into your eyes

into the diving bell
favoring my bad leg
to a snow blown motel
i'm dragging my bad leg

the horizon's heaven's assault
you can live on the salt
you can live on it all

## smoky hands


waiting for an angle of the light
some sound
a certain level of humidity

when memories pile up like snow

if you trip and don't fall on the carnal rug
melting with humility

when weaker people might succumb

## animal

the road spits out a cross and you flip somebody off
see?
this is anarchy

what did i do to get this from you and your
    Tourette's?
you and your static?

you animal
can you cry salty tears?
can you?

Jello on toothpicks
drinking Tang
thanking Jesus for their Rice Krispies

can you dry salty tears?
can you?

## red shoes

this date
this war criminal is brutal
it wants red
so i got red shoes
'cause red becomes you
this red becomes you

eyes closed
you close them in the dark, huh?
what do you think you can't see?

this dance
this war criminal is brutal

# krait

in a suburban desert
a fast food high
we swipe at peeling paint
swat away flies

the crawling milk-fed
squawking, cream-filled hominids
ids
immune to broken
to naked shame
to bolts of lightning

bungee together your body's guards
the bloodiest bond blacking out the dark
the darkest flame
the darkest waltz
a sunburnt snarl thrashing and parched

a singular desire to drive into the dirt
no lust, no gluttony
we're free as algae

those with an all consuming passion in lock step

## soma gone slapstick

he wanted palms
secular psalms

"i'll find you a palm tree
make you think you're in California"

clear lungs
clear lust
soma gone slapstick
you leave only footslips

we all hear the same sound
this whole fall on the rebound

find you smoke: NOLA snow
and we're back in Chicago when i jump out
   the window
your mirror eyes reflecting sky
i did feel sorry for you
overwrought and see-through

a glimmer of the future made this winter
   even crueler

did you know i feel the same?
can you stomach this old dopey game?

a buzzing like a panic made this whole spring
    kinda manic

# between Piety and Desire

incense, strawberry candles and soap
way to butcher a street

there are spells
dizzying spells
you can smell them coming
a torture on the breeze

did you call me?
what did you call me?
trying to turn the other cheek

all clean junkies miss dirty secrets
we're gonna die so what the fuck
we're only here through sheer dumb luck

and we don't like the shit between Piety
   and Desire
we don't like the shit 'cause we belong in it

## colder

they took a picture and from this cold lightning
   living me through
so i feel like an alarm clock

fire came from my mouth is pushing me around
and i'm not loving
i'm not hating
i'm not creating
i'm losing my friends and my young dreams

that was vicious air spilled in my face out
   of love
and out of love

keep walking
if i did the same thing 500 times could you see it
   in the dark?
i trust the weather
i try to make the bodies give me strength
do we see them in the yard?
who cares if they're rolling in bed?
there's only darkness upstairs

does love sit cold 'til you put it somewhere?
do objects spit it at your heart?

i'm colder and colder and colder

## dripping trees


you a clean spark or a twisted parody?
well, look at me


set them to clock time
spit them up at the trees
the dripping trees
these wicked memories


it all comes down eventually

## killing two birds

street puke's not your fault
just walk by it
remember coke falls when it all stopped shining?

you're my nightmare in shining armor
static in the air
everyone like me's a dead man

hold on
i'll buy this in a caffeinated moment
killing two birds with one stone

kissing in a bad rain and exhaust
could be worse, Ms. Hersh, you know where you are
could be worse, Ms. Hersh, you could be lost

numb means nothing hurts me anymore
and i can't feel a thing in my core
i can't feel a thing anymore

i lose you in the street puke and the rain
and if it's not my fault how come i'm dirty?
i'm so hungover i'm ashamed

it's 3:59 and the buzz drills a song home
clean, you dream clean

everyone like me's a nightmare

## long painting

long painting
the air plays along with my chemicals
drained again

and i don't feel so sorry and i don't feel so bad

paralyzed by inaction in a floodlit parking garage
when my mind's as fluid as my body i finally shut up
i'm sorry to say i was in love
static played through my middle
seared my gut

news is bad news
i look to my beer for solace
drained again

## limbo

nice limbo you have here
nice field you have on

baby, go back to your room

you grow the apples around me
i'll spit the seeds in your face
bead me a necklace a decade
i'll wait

i'm gonna run
i'll sweat you
move you to my pores
i'm not gonna cry anymore

dead is next door

# Ginger Park


french fries glisten in the noonday sun
i wouldn't mention this to anyone
where the hell do those sheep think they're going?
soon as i pay up i'm getting out of here

could you leave us alone for just a minute?

lately my life has been flashing before my eyes
lately my life has been passing by
i know i should be concerned about what this means
   but i just keep watching

i don't belong there
i don't belong anywhere
where do think you are?
Ginger Park?

# Arnica Montana

the baby's so simian
i guess we never evolved completely
you can see it in me

a naked grass widow moment
did you see his beautiful eyes in the red
    twilight?

we've done our time in the pressure cooker on
    Arnica Montana
with the desperate
tearing down the highway like they got no place
    to stay

a fulgent fourth grader dressed in nylon and blue
a sheepish smile just for you

we lit our caps and fingernails and leaves behind
    the back porch
through the smoke
four shining eyes
the future's later
everybody's here

## same sun

i broke the payphone when you called
i stole the wire that owned a goddamn piece of you
Ma Bell is not my mother

i can't lie
some bitch gets through and tells the truth

and that's the same sun that burned my mother
that's the same sun on your dashboard
it's the same one on your postcard
i need another

i broke the mirror on your car
i stole the light it had
it tried to take the light from you
it had no color

i can't lie

# Candyland

i lost a boy and now i look for him through every
    window and behind every door
my son went down

this isn't trauma
it's not even drama anymore
i was born with a sad song in my mouth
he gave me a reason to sing it

it's like this boy took all my clear, cold nights
left me hot and dry
and when he falls
i can't hear it

don't wait for pain to find out you exist
don't look for shame
you're better off without it
life is unkind

this isn't Candyland
i know you don't understand
it's so nice not to be ashamed
so nice not to be creeped out

ice is unkind 'til it freezes your enemies
life is unkind 'til it burns up our memories
life is unkind

he gave me a reason to live it

## you cage

you cage, you cage
you can sleep me down

once called from above
i sport your love
i spurn your hotel
i wear your hotel

so you wear ugly hats
you wear them well

i wish the moon wouldn't hang so low
hang over home
hang so

## caffeine

the best of us puking
the rest of us not doing so well
you can tell by the way we look over your shoulder
watching for the next big thing

caffeine in the blood
caffeine on the brain
bad well water
set off a chain reaction
a desperate set of principles

i wish we were lonely
i wish we were boring
it's so much easier

you're driving
and i'm your back seat shadow
the radio keeps playing
the radio keeps saying, "nothing lost and nothing
   gained"

i can soothe you
i feel your heart beating
i hear your soft breathing

## gazebo tree


that sky is ashine with sheen
those eyes are a green machine
spare me your whining in my rainy gazebo tree

deep in my silver pit
the walls are all thick with it
my but you slay me in my rainy gazebo tree

"bless my baby eyes
don't you know Jesus died?
i'm better off inside"

strip and you lose your hide

"what's in that thermos, man?
your female's a garbage can
so you haven't filled her up?
ok, try to fill my cup"

"it's moonshine from cactus"
"well, i guess it can't wreck us"

spare me your moonshining in my raining
    gazebo tree

# vitamins v

4 p.m.
death by mosquito and vitamins v
home and the contrasting squalor
a mouthful of vodka

this lukewarm catastrophe is a recipe for rebirth
or so i overheard

flat on the Afghani carpet
the tub's overflowed
i'm still staring through the fish tank and a
    fistful of Valium

you're gonna wanna keep in touch with your silence
remember shy person hell?
i won't waste your time with lies and there's not
    much truth to tell

you're gonna wanna ride back here with me
i've got the coolest view
and on vitamins v i can't seem to lie to you

## say goodbye

i brought this bottle here for you
can't you drink it?

i brought this body here for you
don't you want it?

say goodbye

i brought this pocketknife for you
don't you use it?

i brought this ball and chain for you
don't you wear it?

## him dancing

him dancing
him rolling on the ground
him moaning
i can't help myself

you be the driver
i can't see no difference in me
you be the cooker
i can't see no difference in me

i'll be the runner
you can love me anyway

# a cleaner light

a high
that's a swell take on this situation i was trying
   to rectify
i was trying to skip out on this high

keep away from the freaks on the fringe
they only talk to you 'cause you give them a good
   excuse to cry

but in a cleaner light it's ok
in a better light it's ok

this strange old sunshine beats me senseless
but it's supposed to be keeping me healthy
it's a lie
you're a strange old thing that keeps me senseless
but you're supposed to be keeping me company

i wake up feeling fragile
it's nothing the tv couldn't cure or lying here
   for my whole life

they only talk to you 'cause you're there

## Mexican women


leave home
blood becomes a foreign substance and see it as
    you let it dry

i forgive my nature or i'll be my saint
i can always feel you in heaven

living in the past
i think if i remember that i'll forget this
i know you will

kill the sky the sun'll fry us
burn the rain we'll die

once there were two Mexican women
ran over the hills
ripped off their skin and ate it up
leave the town for the children
leave their rings to their daughters and fly up

# God's not a dick

chalk it up to circumstance
you watch the tide roll back
it's all over you
it's all over

red and happy
decent deceit bit through the gloom
it's all over you
it's all over
it's riveting, gone and all you got
two black eyes behind sunglasses

tape it all back up
you promise God's not a dick?
New Orleans is on fire with blue flames and
    LA flowers
you promise God's not a dick?

## clay feet

this is no time to fuck up
scooting around the linoleum on all fours
what for again?
better yourself for somebody else

this is no time to wrestle
you're gonna burst a blood vessel
what for again?
we could be falling in love like nobody else

tonight your dream is safe with me
tomorrow we wake up in LA

this is no time to make love
rolling around the linoleum
we fall and we'll fall again
better yourself than somebody else

walking out on clay feet
walking out the long way
what're you gonna say?
what the hell?
what the hell are you gonna say?

tonight your secret's safe with me
tomorrow we wake up in LA
such a lovely dream
what a lovely place

## from the plane

your city looks like campfires from the plane
Lite-Brite cave paintings

dark blue arteries
ice swirls feathering from the plane
you've got ice feather windows
i give
what a nice gesture
though short-lived

spooning sadly
a heart shake
head skipped a beat

# 37 hours

by now i should know where you're going
by now i should but i don't
you're better off wherever you are off to
agile or stoned

by now i should wake you when i'm hungry
right now i should but i'm not
we could be a silkworm tightrope
we should but we're not

i don't want this to be over
you're what i do every day
the only thing that makes any sense
your liver twisting logic far and away the
    smartest thing

and i don't know where i am
plus i don't know when i am
'cause you insist on using fucked up military time
'cause you are better off alone

i've been right here for 37 hours

i dropped a cigarette in my shoe and dove in
    the water
then i swam 'til my hair dreaded
like flying on fire

that day i quit smoking and swimming
i'd heard some advice from above:
ducking under
cramming it in
isn't falling in love

## hips and makers

rocking on the ocean
sucking up the sea
every bird flies over me

we have hips and makers
we have a good time

i married a boxer to keep me from fighting
i married a brewer to keep me from drinking
they keep me dancing

finally it's alright

Unbound is the world's first crowdfunding publisher, established in 2011.

We believe that wonderful things can happen when you clear a path for people who share a passion. That's why we've built a platform that brings together readers and authors to crowdfund books they believe in — and give fresh ideas that don't fit the traditional mould the chance they deserve.

This book is in your hands because readers made it possible. Everyone who pledged their support is listed below. Join them by visiting unbound.com and supporting a book today.

Cyndi Boggs
Stephen Boots
Giorgio Bortoli
Eileen Bowe
Brad Searles /
    Bradley's Almanac
Adie Brown
Mark Brown
Gordon Buchan
Jeoffrey Bull
Jeffrey Burka
Rhiannon Burner
Richard Burton
Steve Buzzard
Erik Calcott
Jon Callas
Penny Carey
Hamilton Carroll
Matt Castanier
Andrew Catlin
John Luke Chapman
Nigel Cheney
Jimmie Chevrier
Brydon Cheyney
Neil Clark
Richard Clemens
John Clifton
Victoria Carter Clowes
Samantha Collett
David Comay
Ian Corless
Alan Coss
Mark Covington
Russell Covington
Chris Cowan
Denise Ann Cox

Crackleford (Band)
Michael Crees
Tony Crowley
Andrew Cundiff
Jarrod Reef Alera
    Cunningham
Stephen Cunningham
David Dale
Geraint Daniel
James Davidson
Paul Davies
Stuart Davies
Divvy Davis
Jef De Pooter
Graham Deakin
Anthony Denny
Megan Denny
Tom Der
Andrew Detchon-Freeth
Aymeric Devoldere
Denise DiGangi
Paul DiGiuseppe
Owen Dixon
Adrian Dörr
Lynsey Anne Downs
Eric Duerr
Tim Duller
Sean Dunham
John Dunn
Lauren Dvorscak
Neil Dyson
Bob Eades
Echo
Matthew Egglestone
Laura Elise
Chris Elliott

Emilio Englade
David Evans
Matthew V Evans
Racheal Everson
Michelle Facey
Michael Fadda
Tracy Farr
Andrea Feldman
Jessica Fisher
Caroline Flanagan
Patrick Ford
John A Fotheringham
Darren Fox
Alan Francis
Michael Frankel
Kevin Garbett
Saffron Uma Gardenchild
Sean Gardner
Andrew Geoghegan
Barry Giglio
Chrissie Giles
Lily-Rygh Glen
Paul Glover
Mara Gold
Leah Good
Christina Goodwin
Eric Goodwin
Jeff Grader
Sander Grootendorst
Kristen Guerin
Susan Guilfoyle
Pål Hagen
Ella & Isabel Hales
Adam Hammond
Richard Hammond
Jack Hankinson

Jonathan Hankinson
Darsha Hardy
Mark Harland
Jennifer Harrelson
Matthew Hart
Luke Hatton
Dirk Haun
Peter Hearn
Jeffrey Hender
Ian Hercus
Dave Hibell
Carey Hiles
Gary Hill
Steven Warren Hill
Molly Cliff Hilts
John Hocking
Tom Homulka
Neil Horabin
Simon Horrocks
Miguel A. Hortiguela
Christine Hughes
Ben Hutchinson
Tom Jackson
Creig Jacobson
Jonathan Jago
Nick James
Craig Janecek
Dan Jenkins
Simon Jennings
Rich John
Dave Johnson
Chris Jones
Dan Jones
Rachel Jones
Philippe Jugé
Steven Kaplan

George! Kazepis
Robert Richard Kegarise
Geoff Kent
Dan Kieran
Michael King
Niamh King
Rachel King
Julie Kinney
Sharon Kirsch
Ken Kline
John Knight
Eric Knoll
Endre János Kovács
Stefan Kumpfmüller
Jason Kurian
Kerry Kwiatkowska
Kay LaFrenais
Gianna LaMorte
Brian Lawlor
Vinh Le
Rory LeBoutillier
Michael Lekas
Ben Lloyd
Phil Locke
David Logue
Katherine Long
Anthony Lorente
David Ludwig
Rachel Lumberg
Gary Lynch
Andrew MacCreary
James Mackay
Calum Macleod
George Magowan
Stephanie Marchesi
Joanne Marino

Vanessa Marley
Luna and Shannon Martin
Karen Martwick
Andrew Mason
Peter Matejic
Mark Matteson
Doug Mayo-Wells
Valerie McAndrews
Sean McArthur
Colm McBriarty
Tony McCulla
Laura McCullough
Eamonn McCusker
Phillip McDonough
Sally McFadyen
Andy McGilvray
Melissa McMasters
Aaron McPherson
David McQuillan
Monica McTighe
Murray P Meador
John Melandro
Natalie Menzies
Adam Mercer
Graham Middleton
Robert Middleton
John Mitchinson
David Morini
Crawford Morris
Maya Castillo Morrison
    and Adam Morrison
Tracey Mullane
Lisa Mullen
Nan Mulrine
Ian Murphy
Paul Murphy

Marta Navarro
Carlo Navato
Louis Neidorf
Nogoj
Jeane E. Norton
Jeff Norton
Garry Nurrish
Hilary Nylander
Riley O'Connor
Paul Oakley
Paulo Oliveira
Daniela Orlando
Antony Osso
Alison Owen
Mark Owen
Rianne P
James E. Pace
Scott Pack
Leigh Pain
Joselle Palacios
Vinnie Part
Lawrence Peachey
Alan Pedder
Louis-Vincent Perrinel
Liz Pesch
Alexander Peterhans
Kelsang Phuntsog
Andrzej Piascik
Matthew Piper
Trevor Pittendreigh
Justin Pollard
Dan Poppe
Suzanne Popper
Richard Potter
Graham Powers
PrettyGreenParrot

Mike Prideaux
Iain Pritchard
Tom Proven
Jonathan Puxley
Andrew Pym
Kenneth Racicot
Rudy Ramos
Kristin Ratcliffe-Hawes
Nicole Reading
Andrew David Reaks
Simon Reekie
Leslie Rich
Rachael Robinson
Alberto Robledo
Glenn Roiz
Rev. Richard Rose
Andy Saavedra
Vicky Salipande
Jarl Salmela
Ben Sansum
Pete Savignano
Gregory Scharpen
Rachel Schedler
Maria Schonert
David Schwartz
Lesley Scott
Paul Scully
Alan Searl
AM Sedivy
Felipe Serrano
Gavin Sheedy
Mark Shoener
Kara Sicotte
Eann Sinclair
Beatrice Sisul
Edward Skawinski

Jane Smith
Jim Smith
Jonathan Smith
Timothy Smith
David Smyth
Shawn Sodersten
Dan Sparks
Richard Stacey
Jenny Staples
Klaas Steenhuis
Timo Stey
Christopher Stow
Nicole Swarts
Steve Taylor
www.themouthmagazine.com
Tim + Norma Thomson
Whitney Thorniley
Mark Tilley
Michael Trinder
Joseph Trombley
Catherine Turley
Ant Turner
Keith Ullrich
Rebecca Utz
Anna van der Stelt
Lien van Gool
Michelle VanSetten
Michael Verzani

Leif Håvard Vikshåland
Katrina Vollentine
Alistair Walder
Grace K. Wallace
Martin Waterman
Steve Watts
Marco Valerio Way
Nadja Weber
Dan Weissman
Adam Weitzman
Nat West
Scott Whipple
Sarah Will
Joshua Willett
Nathan Dean Williams
Clare Wilson
Denise G Wilson
Kirsten Wilson
Francois Wolmarans
Steven Wright
William D Wright
Richard Yandle
Yee
Katherine Mary Zach
Robin L. Zebrowski and
    Joshua Cohen
Fotena Zirps